Rabbids Invasion

RABBIDS INVADE HALLOWEEN

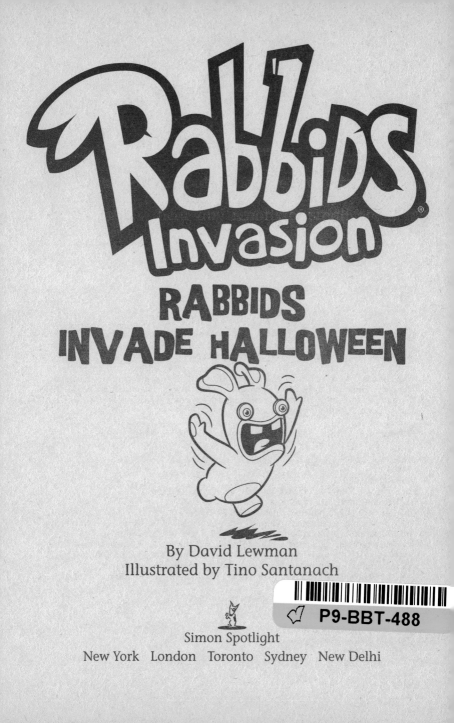

By David Lewman
Illustrated by Tino Santanach

Simon Spotlight
New York London Toronto Sydney New Delhi

This book is a work of fiction. Any references to historical events, real people, or real places are used fictitiously. Other names, characters, places, and events are products of the author's imagination, and any resemblance to actual events or places or persons, living or dead, is entirely coincidental.

Based on the TV series Rabbids™ Invasion as seen on Nickelodeon™

SIMON SPOTLIGHT
An imprint of Simon & Schuster Children's Publishing Division
1230 Avenue of the Americas, New York, New York 10020
This Simon Spotlight paperback edition July 2015
© 2015 Ubisoft Entertainment. All rights reserved. Rabbids, Ubisoft, and the Ubisoft logo are trademarks of Ubisoft Entertainment in the U.S. and/or other countries.
All rights reserved, including the right of reproduction in whole or in part in any form.
SIMON SPOTLIGHT and colophon are registered trademarks of Simon & Schuster, Inc.
For information about special discounts for bulk purchases, please contact
Simon & Schuster Special Sales at 1-866-506-1949 or business@simonandschuster.com.
Designed by Nick Sciacca
Manufactured in the United States of America 0615 OFF
10 9 8 7 6 5 4 3 2 1
ISBN 978-1-4814-4854-3 (hc)
ISBN 978-1-4814-3579-6 (pbk)
ISBN 978-1-4814-3580-2 (eBook)

RABBIDSTEIN!

The scientist looked out the window of the laboratory. Rain splashed against the glass. Lightning flashed in the sky. *CRRRRACK!* Thunder crashed, and the wind howled.

"Wish I had an umbrella," she murmured.

The tall, thin researcher pulled on her coat. "Well, see you tomorrow," she said to her fellow scientist, John. "Don't forget to make sure the Rabbids are locked in. We don't want them getting loose and wandering around the lab again!"

John, a short, balding man with glasses and a mustache, nodded. "Don't worry. I'll remember."

CRRRRACK! John jumped. The thunder was even louder that time!

The woman laughed. "Not scared of a little thunder, are you?" she said, walking out the door.

"Of course not!" John called after her. When he was sure she was gone, he grinned and chuckled. "This is the perfect night for my secret project!"

He unlocked a door and rolled out a long table with wheels.

On the table lay a hideous monster.

It looked like a huge, ugly, black-haired man, but it had green skin, and bolts sticking out of its neck. It lay perfectly still, but it wasn't sleeping.

It was dead.

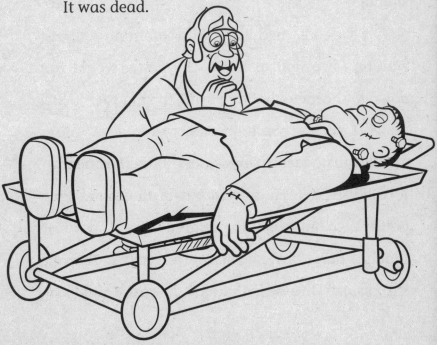

"Tonight," John said to the monster, "you will live! And I'll be the most famous scientist in the world! I'll never have to study Rabbids again!"

The monster said nothing. Because, you know, it was dead.

He quickly attached a metal hat to the monster's head. Wires led from the hat to a big switch on the wall.

"All I need is lots of electrical power," John murmured to himself. "And thanks to this storm, I should get plenty!"

On the roof, he'd installed a lightning rod, just waiting for a bolt to hit it. The power would zap down to the metal hat and bring the monster to life!

At least, that was John's theory.

"But first, I really need to go to the bathroom," John mumbled. He started out of the room, then paused. "What was it she reminded me to do?" He thought hard, but he couldn't remember. Then he shrugged. "Oh, well. I'm sure it wasn't anything important." He hurried off to the bathroom.

Seconds after John left, the door creaked open. Someone poked his head in the room and looked around.

A Rabbid!

"Bwoooooooh," he said when he saw the monster lying on the table. He walked into the room and raised one hand. "Bwah, bwah!" he said.

The monster, still dead, didn't say a thing.

"BWAH, BWAH, BWAH!" the Rabbid yelled. He grabbed the leg of the rolling table and shook it. The table started rolling across the room, straight toward the big switch on the wall. . . .

And at that very moment, a huge bolt of lightning hit the rod on the roof of the laboratory. *CRAAAAACCCKKK!!!*

Power surged through the electrical lines. The table bumped into the switch. *ZZZZZZZZAP!*

The Rabbid watched, fascinated, as the metal hat on the green monster crackled and sparked with blue bolts of electricity.

Slowly, the monster sat up on the table.

"Bwah?" the Rabbid asked. Then he smiled. The big sleeping thing had woken up! Maybe it wanted to play!

"Unnnnhhh," the monster grumbled. It pulled the metal hat off its head. It raised its hands up in front of it, as though it were going to grab someone and strangle them. Then it slid off the table and stiffly walked around the room. *CLOMP! CLOMP! CLOMP!*

"Bwahahahaha!" The Rabbid laughed, clapping his hands. He stuck his arms straight out and started stomping around the room, acting like the monster.

The monster noticed the Rabbid. "Unnnhh?" it said. Laughing, the Rabbid ran right at the monster and butted his head into the monster's leg.

"Unnnh!" the monster cried, afraid of the Rabbid. It tried to hide in a corner of the room, even though it was way too big to hide anywhere.

"Bwuh?" the Rabbid asked, confused. Why should this big monster be afraid of him? He just wanted to play. Maybe if he looked more like the monster . . .

The Rabbid searched the room and found a green marker. He colored his face green. He found two bolts and stuck them to the sides of his neck. Then he found a black marker and drew hair on top of his head.

Satisfied with his new look, the Rabbid faced the monster. He raised his arms and said, "Bwuuunnnh!" doing his best to sound monstrous.

"UUUNNHHH!" screamed the monster, more frightened than ever. Flailing its big arms, it accidentally knocked the door open and ran out of the room.

"Bwah bah!" the Rabbid called after it cheerfully, waving.

He heard footsteps coming down the hall. They didn't sound like the big clomping steps of the monster. Someone else was coming!

The Rabbid didn't want to be put back to bed. What could he do? He looked around the lab frantically. "Bwah, bwah, bwah, bwah!" he said to himself. He spotted the rolling table and quickly climbed up on it. He lay down and closed his eyes.

John burst into the room. He'd heard a lot of strange noises while he was in the bathroom. "What's going on in here?" he shouted.

Then he noticed his monster.

"My creature!" he cried. "It's turned into a . . . Rabbid?"

John crept over to the table and leaned over the Rabbid to examine it closely. The Rabbid sat up and said, "Bhwoo!"

"AAAHHH!" John screamed, startled.

The Rabbid thought that was great.

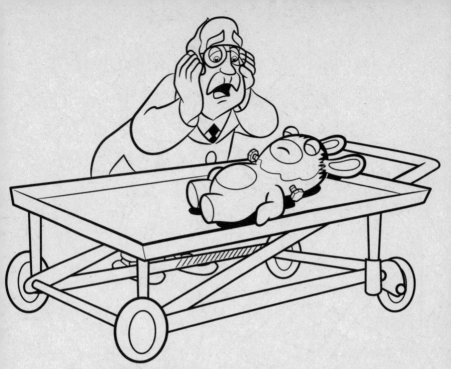

He jumped down off the table and started stomping around the room like the monster again. "Bwhuuunh! Bwhuuunh!"

"Stop!" John said. "You'll break something!"

The Rabbid thought that was a terrific idea.

He stuck his arms straight out and swung them around stiffly. As he stomped around the lab, he crashed into fragile pieces of equipment, knocking them to the floor. *SMASH! BANG! CRASH!*

"BWAAAAAAH!" the Rabbid yelled, having a marvelous time.

"STOP!" John shouted, trying to catch beakers and test tubes before they crashed to the floor. For every one he caught, he missed six.

Finally, John looked up from catching a micro-scope just before it hit the floor. Where was the monster Rabbid?

Disappeared! (He'd gotten tired of playing Monster and gone to get some of his Rabbid friends to see if he could scare them with his monster act. But John had no way of knowing that, because, despite all the time he'd spent studying Rabbids in his lab, he still had no idea what made them tick.)

John wiped his sweaty forehead. He realized he should probably alert the authorities about the mon-ster Rabbid that was on the loose, but he also real-ized he would probably get in a lot of trouble. So he decided to clean up the lab and say nothing. After all, how much damage could one monster Rabbid do?

Meanwhile, the monster Rabbid found his fel-low Rabbids. When they saw his green face, and the bolts on his neck, they wanted to look like that too! So before long there were five Rabbids pretending to be monsters. They went in search of John's monster.

Back in the lab, John was almost finished cleaning everything up when, suddenly, his monster (the big, scary one!) crashed through the door, roaring and growling. It grabbed all the pieces of equipment John had just picked up and hurled them to the floor. *SMASH! SLAM! WHAM!*

John watched helplessly, thinking his night couldn't possibly get any worse. How had his monster changed from a monster to a monster Rabbid and then back into a monster? Before he could try to puzzle out an answer to that riddle, the door to the lab burst open, and five monster Rabbids came in. They saw John's monster and screamed in delight, stomping around the lab and knocking things over trying to "play" with the monster. When the monster tried to hide in the corner again, the Rabbids began throwing test tubes at it to show the monster how much they loved playing this fun game.

It was all too much for John to take. He ran screaming out of the lab and was never, ever heard from again.

And neither was his monster. But the monster Rabbids? They are still out there, of course! So if you hear any reports of small green monsters on the loose in your neighborhood, look out . . . and hide all your breakables!

RABBID OF THE OPERA

Late one night, on the stage of the Grand Opera Hall, a soprano was practicing. "La, la, la, la, la, la, la!" she sang in her beautiful voice.

A man playing the piano stopped playing and looked at his watch. "It's really late," he said. "I think that's enough practicing for tonight."

"But my big audition is tomorrow!" the soprano protested.

"Yeah, and my bedtime is ten minutes from now," the piano player said, standing up, gathering his music, and putting on his coat.

The soprano frowned. "Fine," she snapped. "I'll just stay and practice by myself."

The piano player had already reached the door. He turned back and said, "Are you sure you want to be in here late at night? Alone? They say a phantom haunts the Grand Opera Hall."

The soprano sniffed. "Phantom!" she said, sounding disgusted. "Don't be ridiculous."

"Suit yourself," the man said as he left.

The woman played a note on the piano and started singing again. "La, la, la, la, la, la, la!"

Then . . . *FWOOOOOM!* A deep, loud chord thundered out of the hall's gigantic pipe organ! The soprano jumped.

She peered into the darkness, trying to see who was playing the organ. There seemed to be a small figure sitting on the bench in front of the big keyboard.

"Who's there?" she called. "Are you trying to scare me? This isn't funny!"

After playing three more frightening chords (which sounded like someone just pounding their fists on the keyboard), the small figure on the bench turned around slowly.

It was a Rabbid.

He was wearing a long black cape. Half of his face was hidden by a mask.

"Bwah," he said in a low voice. He climbed down off the bench and walked over to the soprano.

"Who are you supposed to be?" she asked. "The Phantom?"

The Rabbid nodded slowly.

The woman stared at the short figure in the flowing black cape. Then she started to laugh in her high, loud voice. "Ha, ha, ha, ha, ha! The Phantom? You? Absurd!"

The half of the Rabbid's face that was visible scowled. He did *not* like being laughed at. He jabbed one hand into the air.

WHOMP! A heavy sandbag slammed onto the stage right next to the soprano. It had fallen from the rafters high above the stage.

The woman looked frightened. "If that bag had hit me . . . ," she said, shaking. "Did you do that?"

The Rabbid nodded slowly. Then he pointed high above the soprano. She looked up and saw a huge chandelier hanging right over her. She squinted, trying to figure out what it was made of. It looked like . . . toilet plungers?

Was the Rabbid saying that if she didn't do what he said, he'd drop that toilet-plunger chandelier on her?

The Rabbid walked over to the piano. He pulled a long green onion out of his cape and tapped it on the side of the piano.

TAP, TAP, TAP, TAP, TAP! Then he held his hands up like a symphony conductor, using the onion as a baton.

The soprano just stared at him.

The Rabbid waved the onion and his other hand, singing, "Bwah, bwah, bwah, bwah, bwah, bwah, bwah" up and down the notes of a scale. His voice was *not* beautiful.

He gestured to the soprano, as if to say "your turn." When she hesitated, he looked up at the chandelier.

"La, la, la, la, la, la, la," sang the soprano in her beautiful voice.

The Rabbid shook his head violently. He sang again, louder this time. "Bwah, bwah, bwah, bwah, bwah, bwah, bwah!"

"La, la, la, la, la, la, la!"

"BWAH, BWAH, BWAH, BWAH, BWAH, BWAH!"

The angry Rabbid pointed his onion at the toilet-plunger chandelier. The soprano held her hands up with her palms out. "No, no, no!" she pleaded. "I'll try it your way."

She took a deep breath and sang, in the most lovely way possible, "Bwah, bwah, bwah, bwah, bwah, bwah, bwah."

The Rabbid nodded. He gestured with his onion: again.

As the soprano sang her "bwah, bwahs," the Rabbid walked closer to her, staring into her wide-open mouth. He climbed up on the piano to get a closer look. Suddenly, he grabbed her face, opened her mouth even wider, and stared down her throat. She pulled away.

"What are you doing?!" she gasped. "Stop it!"

The Rabbid paced around, thinking. Then he stopped, as though he'd had a brilliant idea. "Bwah hah!" he said.

He pointed to himself, as if to say "try it like this." Opening his mouth wide, he screamed, "BWAAAAAH!"

He pointed to the soprano with his onion.

She shook her head firmly. "I am NOT going to scream! I have an audition for the opera company tomorrow. It's the most important audition of my life. I refuse to ruin my voice by screaming!"

The Rabbid stomped his foot, swirled his cape, and screamed again. "BWAAAAAAAH!"

The soprano glared at him and shook her head slowly.

"Bwah bwah bwah bwah," the Rabbid said, shrugging. It almost seemed as though he were saying, "Have it your way."

He pointed his onion at the toilet-plunger chandelier, and it started to fall!

But the soprano was ready. She sprang into action and ran out of the hall.

CRRRAAAASH! The chandelier hit the stage and burst into a thousand pieces. Toilet plungers flew through the air!

Could the phantom survive such an explosion?

The next morning, the soprano returned to the hall for her audition. "I had the scariest experience last night—" she said to the piano player.

"Tell me later," he interrupted. "You're on."

The soprano smiled a dazzling smile and swept onto the stage. The man she was auditioning for was sitting in the front row.

"For my first number, I'd like to sing . . ."

The man stood up. It was the Rabbid! The Phantom! And he pulled off his mask to reveal . . . HIS TOTALLY NORMAL RABBID FACE UNDERNEATH!

She screamed, "YAAAAAHHH!"

The Rabbid smiled and nodded. *That* was the sound he wanted to hear!

"Bwah bwah bwah bwah!" he said. The soprano wasn't sure, but she thought he meant "You've got the part!"

WERERABBIDS!

Late one evening, three Rabbids ran through a forest. They weren't running away from anything. They were just running because it felt good to run.

One of them pretended to be a plane, sticking his arms out and saying, "Bwummmmm!"

The second one pretended to be a train, chugging his arms in front of him and saying, "BWAH, bwah, bwah, bwah! BWAH, bwah, bwah, bwah!"

The third one . . . Well, it was hard to tell what he was doing. For a while it looked as though he were dancing. Then skipping. Then pretending to swim. All the while he kept singing a bouncy little tune: "Bwah bwah bwah-bwah BWAH!"

As they hurried along, they suddenly heard a different sound. Not a Rabbidy sound. A sound like "Grrrrrrrrr."

A low growl.

In a clearing, they saw a huge wolf standing on a rock. It was staring at them with its red eyes. Its long, sharp teeth were bared. Wolf spit dripped from its teeth.

And it was growling.

"Bwah, bwah, bwah, bwah!" the Rabbids said, delighted to have found a doggy out in the middle of the woods. They loved playing with dogs!

One of the Rabbids picked up a crab apple and tossed it. "Bwah!" he called to the wolf. "Bwah!"

The wolf just stared at him.

The Rabbids looked at one another. How dumb was this dog? It didn't even know how to play fetch!

The second Rabbid decided to show it. He got down on all fours, stuck his tongue out like a dog, and ran over to the crab apple. He picked it up in his mouth, ran back to the first Rabbid, and dropped it on the ground.

He stood up and turned to the wolf, saying, "Bwah bwah! Bwah?" He seemed to be saying something like "Like that! See?"

The third Rabbid picked up the crab apple and tossed it, but the big wolf still just stared at the three Rabbids.

The first Rabbid had had just about enough out of this stupid dog. He marched right over to the wolf, yelled, "Bwah! Bwah, bwah, bwah," and bopped the wolf on the nose.

The wolf didn't like that.

As the Rabbid turned and marched away, the wolf bit him right on the butt.

"BWAAAHHH!" the Rabbid yelled, grabbing his butt. He picked up another crab apple and threw it at the wolf, hitting it on the head. *Bonk!*

The other two Rabbids thought Throw Stuff at the Dog looked like a splendid game. They hurled rocks, pinecones, and anything else they could find (even one unfortunate toad) at the wolf.

As the toad hopped away, the wolf thought about eating the Rabbids. Would they be tasty? Tender? Sweet and satisfying? The wolf decided the Rabbids didn't look all that yummy, so it jumped down off the rock and disappeared into the gloom.

But as the Rabbids would soon find out, it wasn't just an ordinary wolf. . . .

Later that night, the Rabbids found a comfy spot in some nice soft grass to snuggle down and go to sleep. Just as they were settling down, though, the moon came up—a big, bright, full moon.

"Bwah, bwah, bwah, bwah!" complained one of

the Rabbids. The moon was making it so light out that it would be hard to sleep. They covered their eyes with their stubby arms as best they could.

The Rabbid who had been bitten on the butt started to itch. He scratched his butt. He scratched his feet. And he scratched his head. He itched all over!

As the other two Rabbids watched in amazement, thick, dark hair started to grow all over their itchy friend! Soon he was completely covered in dark-brown fur! His two teeth grew long points! He hunched over, held his hairy paws in front of him, and gave a low growl.

Then he threw back his head and howled. "BWOOOOOOOH!"

He had turned into . . . A WERERABBID!

The other two Rabbids stared at the Wererabbid.
They looked at each other. They looked back at their
friend and pointed.

"BWAHAHAHA!"

The Wererabbid growled louder. But the other two Rabbids just laughed even harder. They thought the furry Rabbid looked hilarious. All that dark hair! Those red eyes! Those long, pointy teeth! Hilarious!

"BWAHAHAHAHA!"

The Wererabbid didn't like being laughed at. He jumped off the rock and ran straight toward the two Rabbids with his mouth open wide.

"BWRRRRRR!" he growled.

"BWAAAAAH!" they yelled as they took off running through the forest.

The Wererabbid loped after them, picking up speed as he went. Leaves crunched and twigs snapped under his hairy paws. Small woodland creatures ducked down into their burrows as he ran by.

In hardly any time at all, the Wererabbid had caught up with the two Rabbids. With a loud roar, he leaped through the air, grabbed one of them, and sank his fangs into his butt.

"BWOW!" the Rabbid yelled, clutching his bitten butt.

Under the light of the full moon, the second Rabbid sprouted fur all over his body. His eyes turned red, and his two teeth grew into long, sharp fangs.

He too was a Wererabbid!

Now the two Wererabbids turned and stared at the last Rabbid. He gulped. Then he ran.

He tried dodging around boulders. He climbed over fallen trees. He even waded through shallow streams trying to get away from the two Wererabbids.

But there was no escape. Before long he was caught, bitten, and turned into a Wererabbid.

Now there were three.

The Wererabbids looked at one another. They grinned. They were all Wererabbids . . .

. . . and they loved it! They ran through the forest, enjoying the speed and power of their Wererabbid legs!

The Wererabbids saw the light of a campfire flickering in a clearing. They bounded into the clearing, growling and snapping their long, sharp teeth. Whoever was lying around that campfire was going to get a terrifying surprise!

But the campfire belonged to three other Rabbids. They sat up and stared at the three Wererabbids. Then they started to do something the Wererabbids hadn't expected. . . .

"BWAHAHAHAHA!"

They laughed! They pointed at the Wererabbids and laughed hysterically! The Rabbids thought the furry Wererabbids were the funniest thing they'd ever seen.

The Wererabbids looked at one another. They weren't terrifying. They were a joke!

The Wererabbids huddled together. They were going to pluck one another's long fur out so they wouldn't look funny anymore. They grabbed one another's fur and yanked. . . .

"BWOOOUUUCH!" That really hurt.

They gave up and fell asleep with the Rabbids still laughing at them.

But the next morning, after the moon went down and the sun came out, the Wererabbids turned back into regular Rabbids. "Bwah." They sighed, relieved that they no longer looked ridiculous.

But now, once a month, when the moon is full, they change back into fierce, hairy Wererabbids! If you ever meet them in the deep, dark woods, remember: JUST LAUGH AT THEM!